ThunderTrucks! is published by Stone Arch Books
a Capstone imprint
1710 Roe Crest Drive
North Mankato, Minnesota 56003
www.mycapstone.com

Cataloging-in-Publication Data is available on the
Library of Congress website.

ISBN: 978-1-4965-5735-3 (library hardcover)
ISBN: 978-1-4965-5739-1 (eBook)

Summary: The B-PHON monster truck takes on his
toughest competition — himself!

Designed by Brann Garvey

Printed in Canada
010797S18

THUNDERTRUCKS!

COLOSSAL

COURSE!

BY BLAKE HOENA

ILLUSTRATED BY FERN CANO

STONE ARCH BOOKS
a capstone imprint

CONTENTS

CHAPTER ONE

A small, rookie truck named B-phon

rolls into Trolympia. It is his first visit to

the capital.

"Wow! This city is huge," he honks.

All around him, trucks zoom through

the streets. They honk excitedly. **HONK!**

HONK! They beep loudly. **BEEP! BEEP!**

"What's all the excitement about?"

B-phon asks.

The other trucks ignore him. They just zip on by.

VWOOOOSH!

"Where is everyone going?" B-phon tries to ask.

The streets are crowded, but notruck pays him any attention. B-phon is simply a small truck in a big city.

Above him, he spots helicopters whirling about. They follow the crowd of trucks toward the center of the city.

If only I could fly, B-phon thinks. *I could see what is going on.*

B-phon watches as more and more trucks zoom down the street. Then he hears sometruck beep, "Perseus is making a surprise visit!"

Perseus is a famous ThunderTruck! He raced Medusa in the World Endur-X Challenge.

Another truck honks, "I think Theseus is coming!"

Theseus challenged Bulltastic to race through the endless Monster Maze!

Then a truck asks, "Is Hercules going to be there too?"

Hercules was the first ThunderTruck to complete the Rough & Tough Twelve!

"Wow!" B-phon beeps. "My three favorite hero trucks!"

B-phon wants to be famous like Perseus, Theseus, and Hercules. He wishes he were half as famous as them — or even a teeny, tiny bit as famous.

B-phon also wishes he had a special power. All ThunderTrucks have one.

Perseus can leap higher and farther than any other truck. Theseus can outthink and outsmart all other trucks. Hercules is the mightiest truck on Earth!

But B-phon, all he knows how to do is get covered with dust and mud.

As trucks speed by, they splatter B-phon with mud. They kick up clouds of dust that cause him to choke and cough.

"I want – **COUGH! COUGH!** – to go to – **COUGH! COUGH!**" he coughs.

B-phon joins the crowd. He follows the other trucks as they stream into the pit. It is a huge monster truck arena in the center of the city. Trucks fill up the stands.

On the track below, B-phon spots Perseus and Theseus.

Trucks beep, **"Perseus! Perseus!"**

Trunks honk, **"Theseus! Theseus!"**

"Where is Hercules?" some trucks rumble.

Slowly, the rumbles become louder than the beeps and honks.

"Hercules needs a tune up after completing the Rough & Tough Twelve," Perseus says.

"So he won't be joining us today," Theseus adds.

The rumbles turn to disappointed exhausts.

"But we have exciting news!" Perseus continues.

"One of you can join us on an adventure!" Theseus adds.

All the trucks in the stands get quiet.

"We have been challenged to a race by the Chimera Brothers," Perseus says.

B-phon has heard of the Chimera Brothers monster trucks. One is called The Goat and another The Lion. The last one is The Dragon! They are some of the scariest monster trucks around. They have turned everyone they have raced into rust buckets!

"There are three of them, and only two of us," Theseus adds.

B-phon hears a rumble in the crowd.

"We will face The Goat," Perseus says. "He can ram a truck hard enough to knock all four tires off with one blow."

Around B-phon he hears the revving
of engines.

"We will face The Lion," Theseus says.
"With his spiked bumpers, he can tear your
fenders off."

B-Phon hears tires screeching.

"Lastly is The Dragon," Perseus says.

"He shoots flames from his grill!"

"If you survive getting rammed by The Goat and The Lion," Theseus says. "The Dragon will fry you!"

B-phon can barely hear the heroes speak with the engines revving and tires screeching all around him.

"Who would like to face the Chimera

Brothers with us?" Perseus asks.

Silence.

B-phon looks around. He is alone in

the stands.

"You're our third

racer!" Theseus

shouts to B-phon.

CHAPTER TWO

PERSEUS GETS PUMMELED

The next day, B-phon rolls out of Trolympia with the two famous heroes.

"I can't believe it," he says. "I'm going on an adventure!"

Perseus and Theseus look at each other.

"Will there be danger?" B-phon asks. "Will we risk bumper and fender?"

Perseus and Theseus both sigh.

B-phon is excited. He can't stop talking.

"Have you raced the Chimera Brothers before?" he asks. "Which one scares you the most?"

He does not get an answer. The heroes speed ahead. They ignore B-phon and talk about their past adventures.

"Remember that time we raced against Jason?" Perseus says.

"I can't believe he won the Golden Fenders," Theseus replies.

As the heroes relive past adventures, B-phon worries about his future adventure.

Many trucks have taken up the Chimera Brothers' challenge. Most of them were turned to heaps of scrap.

"Do we have a plan?" B-phon asks. "How can we beat the Chimera Brothers?"

SCREEECH! The two heroes skid to a halt. They glance back at B-phon.

"Everything will be fine," Perseus says.

"We're ThunderTrucks, and ThunderTrucks always win," Theseus adds.

Then they turn and continue on.

"How much farther?" B-phon asks. "Wouldn't it be quicker if we could fly there?"

The ThunderTrucks ignore him as they climb up a hill. Below is the Chimera's Brothers' racetrack. It is filled with obstacles, from mud pits to jumps over smashed wrecks and steep berms.

"Wow!" B-phon says. "That looks dangerous. Doesn't that look dangerous?"

Perseus and Theseus don't reply. They head down the other side of the hill.

"Here they come," The Lion roars.

"Who's that with them?" The Goat bleats.

"Doesn't matter," The Dragon snorts. "He's toast!"

B-phon and the two ThunderTrucks roll up to the evil monster trucks. "Remember what we are racing for?" The Lion asks.

"Winners get the losers' engines," Theseus says.

"After we are through with you," The Goat begins.

"You will never race again," The Dragon finishes with a snort.

B-phon gulps. He saved up all of his allowance just to buy his Soarin' V6 engine. He doesn't want to risk losing it. But it's too late to back out now.

"Everytruck get ready!" An official suddenly blares.

B-phon rolls up to the starting line with
the ThunderTrucks and evil monster trucks.

"Set!"

Engines rev.

"GO!"

Tires spin,
kicking up dirt.

The Dragon shoots a blast of fire at
B-phon. He swerves to avoid it and spins off
the track.

In last place, B-phon watches Theseus
speed off, taking the lead.

Then he sees The Lion nipping at Perseus'
tires. Perseus tries to leap out of the way. As
he does, The Goat rams into him.

Perseus lands on his side in the middle of the track with a loud **THUD!**

The Dragon rolls up to Perseus. Smoke and flames pour out from his grill. He is about to roast Perseus!

CHAPTER THREE

THESEUS GETS THUMPED

"*NOOOOOO!*" B-phon screams.

He jumps back onto the track. With

dust flying, he speeds toward Perseus.

B-phon swerves into The Dragon with a

THUMP!, just as the monster lets loose a

blast of flame. It blackens the ground

beside Perseus.

As the Chimera Brothers race after Theseus, B-phon pushes Perseus onto his tires.

"You saved me," Perseus says.

"Can you continue the race?" B-phon asks.

Perseus sputters forward, limping badly.

"I think I cracked an axle," he says. "You need to go help Theseus."

"But how?" B-phon asks. "I'm not a ThunderTruck. I don't even have a special power."

"Everytruck has a special power," Perseus says. "Now go!"

B-phon rejoins the race as Perseus limps off the track.

B-phon speeds over jumps. He bucks and spins through a mud pit. He darts around spike-covered barriers.

Up ahead, he sees the Chimera Brothers. B-phon is catching up to them. But something is odd. They aren't going very fast.

Then Theseus races up behind him. **"I'm lapping you!"** he shouts as he zooms by B-phon.

Then B-phon understands what is happening. The Chimera Brothers aren't trying to catch up to Theseus. They are waiting to ambush him.

"Stop!" B-phon shouts.

But Theseus speeds away. He jumps over ramps. He spins through mud pits. He darts around spike obstacles.

B-phon races after Theseus. But he is not quick enough to catch the ThunderTruck.

B-phon watches as Theseus darts by The Dragon. He easily passes The Lion. But when he tries to get by The Goat, The Goat cuts him off.

Theseus swerves to avoid crashing into The Goat. As he does, The Lion sneaks up behind him. He nips at Theseus' back tires with his spiked front bumper.

POP!
POP!
POP!

Theseus' tires explode. He spins out in the middle of the track.

The Goat stops and turns around. He revs

his engine. His tires spin. Then he charges

Theseus. VROOOOOOM!

CRACK!

"Ooh! Ow! Oh. Ouch!"

Theseus groans as he tumbles down

the track.

He lands on his side.

The Dragon rolls up to him. He revs his

engine and smoke pours out from his hood.

Theseus is about to get fried!

B-phon speeds forward as fast as he

can. As The Dragon starts to shoot flames,

B-phon bumps into him. The Dragon misses

and scorches the ground next the Theseus.

"You are toast," The Dragon snarls at B-phon. Then he races off.

B-phon rolls up to Theseus. He nudges the hero's tires.

"Are you okay?" B-phon asks.

"I don't think so," he sputters. Smoke pours out from under his hood. "I think I popped a piston or two."

B-phon pushes Theseus off the track.

"It is up to you to win this race," Theseus says.

"But I'm not a ThunderTruck!" B-phon says. "And I told you, I don't even have a special power."

"Yes, you do, B-phon," Theseus says.

"You just haven't needed it yet."

Then B-phon speeds off.

CHAPTER FOUR

THREE ON ONE

B-phon now has two goals. One: He has to win the race. Two: He has to survive.

Surviving is probably more important and more difficult. But if he loses, he more than loses. Then Chimera Brothers get his engine. A truck can't do much without one.

B-phon revs his engine. His tires spin. Dirt flies. He races after the Chimera Brothers. He leaps over jumps. He zooms over berms.

But the brothers don't appear to be racing. They putter along the track, and B-phon easily catches up to them.

Then they stop, blocking his path.

"Hey, it's the hero wannabe," The Goat bleats.

"Careful or you might get hurt," The Lion roars.

"Or burnt to a crisp!" The Dragon snorts.

B-phon is not sure what to do. The brothers are in his way. And he saw what happened to Theseus when he tried to pass them.

The Goat charges. B-phon darts to the side. The Goat clips his back fender.

Next The Lion pounces. B-phon darts to the other side. The Lion scratches the other side of the back fender.

B-phon is left facing The Dragon. Smoke pours out from under his hood. B-phon knows what's coming next. But instead of running away from The Dragon, he charges.

When fire starts to erupt from The Dragon's grill, B-phon shoots up a ramp.

B-phone soars over the flames. But his underside gets a little scorched.

He lands on the other side of The Dragon with a **THUMP!**

Suddenly, B-phon finds himself in the lead. But the three Chimera Brothers are now mad.

"He got away from us," The Goat bleats.

"We can't let him win," The Lion roars.

"It is **SUPER MONSTER** time!" The Dragon snorts.

Super Monster —

what is that?

B-phon wonders.

He glances back, and what he sees scares him. As the Chimera Brothers race after B-phon, they join together. First The Goat rams into The Lion. Then The Dragon rams into The Goat and The Lion.

Their parts jumble together. The three monster trucks suddenly become one Super Monster truck!

The Super Monster has spiked bumpers like The Lion. It has ramming horns like The Goat. It also shoots flames from its grill like The Dragon. But that is not the worst of it. The Super Monster is three times as big and twice as fast, and it is catching up to B-phon.

CHAPTER FIVE

FLYING HIGH

"I could use a superpower right about now," B-phon mutters to himself.

The Super Monster is hot on his bumper. B-phon can feel his fiery breath. He can see his ramming horns getting close. And he worries about the Super Monster's spiked bumpers too.

B-phon cannot outrace the Super Monster. So he slams on his brakes and skids to a stop. The Super Monster zips past. He does a 180 in the middle of the track to face B-phon.

"You are scrap," he rumbles.

His engine roars and his tires spins. The Super Monster speeds toward B-phon. Not knowing what else to do, B-phon rushes at him.

B-phon hopes to dart past the large truck. But as he veers to the right, Super Monster tries to cut him off.

B-phon is forced up and over a berm. He expects to crash off the track.

But the unexpected happens!

"Hey, I can fly," B-phon shouts. "I've always wanted to fly!"

B-phon spreads his doors and whirls around.

The Super Monster shoots flames at him.

But B-phon ducks and dives out of the way.

Then he swoops and spins around the

Super Monster. All the while, the bigger

truck tires to fry him.

Soon every ting around the Super

Monster is on fire.

"Hey, I'm trapped!" it cries.

Then it starts to shake in fear. It shakes so hard, that it falls apart, and the Chimera Brothers fall to the ground.

B-phon glides down the to track. He speeds toward the finish line. The ref truck waves the checkered flag.

Suddenly, B-phon is surrounded by three hero trucks. Hercules is with Perseus and Theseus.

"You did it!" Perseus shouts.

"You're a hero!" Theseus shouts.

"Sorry I'm late," Hercules says. "But it looks like you didn't need me."

From down the track, they hear loud coughing and sputtering. The three Chimera Brothers limp and wheeze toward the finish line. Their tires are flat. Smoke pours out of their engines. And they are covered in black scorch marks.

"You won the race," Perseus says.

"You can take their engines,"
Theseus adds.

"Nah, I think I'll keep my Soarin' V6,"
B-phon says.

Just then, all four of The Goat's tires fall off. He lands on the ground with a **THUMP!** All of The Lion's fenders rattle to the ground. Then The Dragon crumples to a pile of ash.

"Look who's toast now!" B-phon says with a laugh.

BELLEROPHON AND THE CHIMERA

Colossal Course! is based on the Greek myth of Bellerophon and the Chimera.

Bellerophon, or B-phon for short, was a famous Greek hero. His father was Poseidon, god of the sea.

While traveling through the land of Lycia, Bellerophon heard stories of the fearsome Chimera. This monster had the head and body of a lion. A goat's head stuck up from its back. At the tip of its tail was the head of a fire-breathing dragon.

The Chimera was destroying people's homes and burning their villages. Bellerophon hoped to put an end to the monsters' destruction. But he had no idea how to defeat the horrible beast. He could not get close to it because of its fiery breath.

But luckily Bellerophon had help with his quest. Athena, goddess of wisdom, told him how to capture Pegasus. Pegasus was a winged-horse.

Riding Pegasus, Bellerophon was able to fly above the Chimera's deadly flames and the monsters razor-sharp claws. Then he tossed a spear at the beast, killing it.

The land of Lycia was saved!

BLAKE HOENA

Blake Hoena grew up in central Wisconsin, where he wrote stories about robots conquering the moon and trolls lumbering around the woods behind his parents' house. He now lives in St. Paul, Minnesota, with his wife, two kids, a dog, and a couple of cats. Blake continues to make up stories about things like space aliens and superheroes, and he has written more than 70 chapter books and graphic novels for children.

FERN CANO

Fernando Cano is an illustrator born in Mexico City, Mexico. He currently resides in Monterrey, Mexico, where he works as a full-time illustrator and colorist at Graphikslava Studio. He has done illustration work for Marvel, DC Comics, and role-playing games like Pathfinder from Paizo Publishing. In his spare time, he enjoys hanging out with friends, singing, rowing, and drawing.

GLOSSARY

arena (uh-REE-nuh) — a large area or building that is used for sports or entertainment

axle (AK-suhl) — a rod in the center of a wheel, around which the wheel turns

grill (GRIHL) — the front grate on a vehicle

berm (BERM) — a shelf or path at the top or bottom of a slope

fender (FEN-dur) — a protective guard over a wheel of an automobile, motorcycle, or bicycle

obstacle (OB-stuh-kuhl) — something that gets in the way or prevents someone from doing something

piston (PISS-tuhn) — a small cylinder that moves back and forth in a larger cylinder inside a vehicle engine

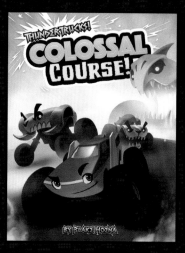
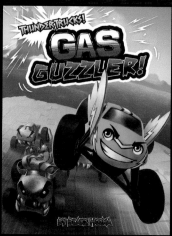